W9-CDD-479

FOR EAGLE EYES ONLY

by Rolf Heimann

Watermill Press
Mahwah, N.J.

First published in USA by Watermill Press
Mahwah, New Jersey.
Produced by Joshua Morris Publishing Inc. in association with
The Five Mile Press
Copyright © 1988 Rolf Heimann
Printed in USA

ISBN 0-8167-2202-1

You don't really need a magnifying glass to solve any of the problems in this book. But you do need sharp eyes and some time and patience. After you have found all the things which the stories ask for, read the last pages and start all over again!

The king was furious. He had ordered his cook to bake him four blackberry pies, but when he came to pick them up there were only three left.

"I'm sorry," explained the cook, "I went down to the cellar and when I came back, one pie was gone."

The king cried: "Bring all the servants who've been in the kitchen today. I will question them."

The servants assembled. All of them said they were innocent.

The maid said she was on a diet, the cleaning woman said she hated blackberry pie, the coachman said he had only come for a drink of water and the kitchen boy said he wouldn't dare take anything, not after the beating he was given last time, when he had taken a tiny crust of stale bread.

"Silence!" screamed the king. "As you know, I'm a reasonable man. But it's not just the pie, it's the principle. First you steal my pie, then you tell me a pack of lies. I won't have that in my castle. If none of you will tell me who the thief is I'll have all your heads chopped off and I mean it."

Could you save the lives of the servants? Look carefully and you'll find the thief.

Karl called to his sister: "Hurry up, I can hear the ice cream van!"

The ice cream van passed the camping ground only once every day, and the children hated to miss it. "Wait for me!" cried Selena. "Mom, where are my thongs?"

The path was full of prickles and Selena did not want to go barefoot. Selena's mom did not know where her daughter's thongs were.

"It's about time you learned to take care of your things," she said.

"They're your thongs after all. Don't expect me to find them for you.

"And hurry up, or you'll miss out on the ice cream…"

Selena was in trouble. Their camp was a jumble of things, but with sharp eyes one can spot the two thongs.

Ben Gibson, chief engineer of the interstellar supply depot Trivia III came racing up the hill on his jet crawler. "I've got good news and bad news," he called out.
"The bad news is that this planet is about to explode. The good news is that Smithy is nearly finished with the repairs on our escape module."
"You call that good news?" cried the workers in alarm. "Why, we should have left days ago!"
"I'm glad you understand how serious the situation is," answered the chief engineer, "because I want you to find another one of these for the starboard engine. It's a binary flow control duct for the secondary combustion chamber. Smithy threw one out the other day but now we need it. The sooner you find it, the earlier we'll be able to get away."

Chief engineer Gibson was right: Trivia III was about to blow up. But if the missing part is found in time, the crew can still get away. Don't stop until you find it! Every second counts!

Caitlin Mason, police helicopter pilot, directed her machine towards the city's biggest bank building. She had received a radio message saying that armed bandits had stolen half a million dollars and escaped in a green car.

"A green car!" called co-pilot Hanna Smith in despair. "Why, there must be hundreds of green cars in the city. We have no hope of finding the right one!"

"We just might have," said pilot Mason. "The car in question also has red wheels. There can't be many cars like that around."

If the helicopter crew can spot the getaway car and radio its position to the ground, police can put up roadblocks, set off in pursuit and arrest the bank robbers. And if the crew's eyes are as good as yours they're bound to find the car pretty soon!

It had been described as the wedding of the year.
Sylvia Wheatherton-Smyth, third cousin to the Earl of Worcestershire, was to be married to Freddie Bloggs, heir to a million-dollar tomato sauce empire. All the newspapers and television stations had sent their reporters.
But when it was time to put the ring onto the bride's finger, the ring could not be found. Both the groom and the best man turned their pockets inside out. There was no ring.
The guests at the back craned their necks and those in front began to giggle.
Sylvia Wheatherton-Smyth blushed with embarrassment. She hissed: "I've never been so humiliated. If you don't find the ring within one minute, the wedding's off. I'd rather stay single than marry such a fool."

You have spotted the ring already, haven't you?

6

Ranger Ashley Stunnenberg felt like crying. He had been sent into the Grand Canyon to do a survey on the wildlife, but just as he'd started to count the little gray squirrels, his burro had bolted and left him without any of his equipment. He felt like a fool! Whatever would he do without his binoculars and his notebook? How could he survive without his water canteen, his flour and his blanket? And his favorite frying pan, the one with the brown handle, was gone too.

What should Ashley do? If only he could find his burro again, or at least the six most important pieces of his equipment.

"I'm hungry," said Werner as soon as his father had stopped their car at the side of the road. "Look, there's a fish restaurant. Let's go and have fish and chips!"

"I don't like fish," objected his sister Ina. "Let's have chicken. There's a chicken place over there!"

"Why do you always have to disagree?" asked their father. "Before we do anything else I will have to find a gas station. I think I see one already—we'll have to take the first road to the right. After I fill up we'll go and eat, and we'll go to the first restaurant we come to. No arguments."

"Just watch these roads," their mother pointed out. "Some of them are one-way streets."

Will they have fish or chicken for dinner?

Once upon a time, deep in the foothills of the Himalayas there lived two children called Yack and Yill. One day Yack became very ill and his sister went to the local healer.

"I'm afraid," said the wise old man, "there is nothing I can do for your brother. To save him we need a certain herb which grows in a very special place up in the mountains. It's called *superfluensis floribundis,* or redwort for short. Alas, I'm too old and feeble to make the journey to get it."

"I'll get it! I'll get it!" cried Yill. "Just tell me where to find it and what it looks like!"

"I can do better than that," said the healer. "Here, take this picture."

When Yill arrived at the place in the mountains she was amazed at the variety of plants. Will she find the herb which could save her brother? It will be dark soon and there is no time to lose. Help her and you'll have a friend for life!

"Grandmother," cried Little Red Riding Hood, "why do you have such small eyes? And such a small nose? And such tiny ears?"

"What do you expect?" asked her grandmother, eyeing the basket which the girl had brought with her. "And speak up, I can hardly hear you. My ears are only human, you know."

"And why do you have such a small mouth, without any teeth in it at all?" shouted Little Red Riding Hood at the top of her voice.

"Hush, my girl, not so loud! Do you want the wolf to hear us? By the way, have you seen him today?"

"No, I haven't," answered the girl.

"Well, go and find him. Tell him I left a dish of oatmeal in the garden for him. You see, I don't like it at all when he walks around hungry; there's no telling what he might get up to."

Help Little Red Riding Hood find the wolf. He's somewhere in the woods!

Elisa and Vincent were having a picnic at their favorite spot when they heard a big splash in the water. They looked up and could not believe their eyes. "What is it?" cried Vincent in amazement. "Is it a dragon? Or the Loch Ness Monster?" "It could be a dinosaur or something," said Elisa. "And look what it has done to our boat! We'll get the blame for it, for sure. What are we going to do?"

"Nobody is going to believe us," agreed Vincent, "unless we take a photograph. Where is our camera?" They knew they had brought a camera, but in the excitement they could not remember where they had put it.

In a few minutes the monster will slip back into the water, never to appear again. Is that enough time to find the camera?

"Did you see Ginger?" asked Laura. "I can't find him anywhere!"

Laura's father, who was about to shovel the freshly fallen snow away, paused in his work. "He can't be far," he said. "Have you looked in the kitchen?"

"I looked everywhere," Laura cried. "The poor thing will freeze to death if he's outside. It's so cold today." Ginger was Laura's kitten, and she loved him more than anything else in the world.

"Why don't you go and check the upstairs window?" suggested Laura's father. "You know how Ginger loves jumping out onto the roof of the woodshed."

If Ginger had indeed jumped out of the upstairs window, his tracks should be visible in the fresh snow. Follow those paw prints now, before the snow is cleared away!

The pirate captain was grinning from ear to ear. He and his men had not only captured rich treasure, but also a little boy called Ernest. Ernest happened to be the son of the captain's worst enemy.

"You, my boy," growled the pirate, "shall be shark bait ere the sun goes down!"

"Captain, sir," said Ernest trying to conquer his fear, "you ought to ask me a riddle, as a chance to save my life. It would be the fair thing to do, sir."

"Fair, eh!" roared the captain, swishing his murderous blade through the air. "I know no riddles, but I do like to be fair. I tell you what—if you can guess the name of my parrot you shall go free. What's more, if you guess right you can have all the pieces of eight in my treasure chest."

"You must give me a hint," begged Ernest.

"Very well, here's a hint: my parrot's name is like my dog's name, only backwards!" Since his dog had a very unusual name the captain was confident that his prisoner would never guess correctly.

Little Ernest thanked his lucky stars that his glasses were not broken during his capture. His sharp eyes saved his life. Would you be able to save yours?

Tatsuo's birthday party had been a great success. All his friends and relatives had come and he'd never had so many presents!

"You must write them all a thank you note," his mother reminded Tatsuo after all the guests had gone. "I will," said Tatsuo and grabbed his notebook, then surveyed his presents with embarrassment. "Oh dear, now I'm not quite sure just who gave me what…" His sister Yuki had a good idea. "Just match the wrapping paper and packages with the presents. That way you can work out where they all came from!"

Yuki's idea was a good one. But is it still possible to find the matching wrapping paper?

If you've come this far you have done well. Let's see if you're just as quick in answering the next set of questions!

In the silence which followed the king's threat one could suddenly hear a slurping and licking and chewing and gnashing of teeth. It came from behind the oven where the dog was eating the missing pie! The servants were relieved that the culprit had been found. Luckily the dog happened to be one of the king's favorites and wasn't punished too harshly.

But the cook's troubles were not over yet. After the king had eaten the three remaining pies he got indigestion and asked for his medicine. Could the bottle be found before the king became angry again? The cook had forgotten where he had put it, but he remembered that it was a brown bottle with a red and green label.

It took Selena some minutes to find her sandals: one was in the back of the car, the other one in the tent. During her search she also found the two fishing hooks her father had lost and her little sister's missing hairbrush. (Can you see them too?)

Selena was just about to rush after her mother when Karl came back, calling breathlessly, "Mom forgot her money. It's in the brown bag with the green handle!"

Fortunately Selena remembered seeing it in her search. Do you?

Luckily they found the missing part soon enough. It was near cart No. 6. Suddenly the chief engineer discovered another problem. He noticed that in the excitement, the hoses to the fuel tank had become entangled. If fuel A was ever put into tank B there could be a disaster. Better check the hoses right away, before it is too late!

"I can see it," pilot Mason called excitedly into the microphone. "A vehicle answering the description is proceeding north along the river. It's just going under the bridge."

Within a few minutes the police on the ground had stopped the getaway car and arrested the bandits.

"Well done," came the message through the radio, "return to base."

"While we're up here," suggested co-pilot Smith, "let's look for my neighbor's lost dog."

"No way," laughed pilot Mason. "We can't waste our time looking for lost dogs! You ought to know what it costs to keep this machine in the air. Besides, we'd never recognize it from up here."

"Sure we would. It is a black dog with a brown tail—very unusual. Why, look! I have spotted it already!"

"There is a notorious jewel thief among the guests," whispered Detective Sergeant Mary Lyndon to her assistant Dennis Dumbos.

"Now why would they invite a jewel thief?" wondered Dumbos aloud. "He came uninvited of course," hissed Lyndon, "and he's fiendishly clever. He usually hides stolen rings in flowerpots. So when he's searched, he's clean."

"How do you know it's a he?" asked the assistant cunningly. He always tried to be one step ahead. "It could be a woman, you know."

"He's said to be bald," snapped the detective. "And we know he always wears a red tie and white carnation. So go and arrest him!"